# The Berenstain Bears' COMIC VALENTINE

Copyright © 1998 by Stan & Jan Berenstain.
All rights reserved. Published by Scholastic Inc.
CARTWHEEL BOOKS and the CARTWHEEL BOOKS logo
are trademarks and/or registered trademarks of Scholastic Inc.

Library of Congress Cataloging-in-Publication Data

Berenstain, Stan, 1923-
    The Berenstain bears' comic valentine / Stan & Jan Berenstain.
        p.    cm.
    "Cartwheel books."
    Summary: Brother Bear wonders who has been sending him secret
valentines, but he does not discover the identity of his admirer until he meets the
goalie of the opposing team after his big championship hockey game.
    ISBN 0-590-94729-X
    [1. Valentine's Day — Fiction.   2. Hockey — Fiction.   3. Bears — Fiction.
4. Stories in rhyme.]   I. Berenstain, Jan, 1923-   II. Title.
PZ8.3.B4493Bhb    1998
[E] — dc21                                                                          97-2076
                                                                                        CIP
                                                                                         AC

                        10  9  8  7  6  5  4  3  2  1

Printed in the U.S.A.

First printing, January 1998

# The Berenstain Bears' COMIC VALENTINE

# Stan & Jan Berenstain

Cartwheel
·B·O·O·K·S·®

SCHOLASTIC INC.
New York  Toronto  London  Auckland  Sydney

**FEBRUARY**

| | | | | 1 | 2 | 3 |
|---|---|---|---|---|---|---|
| 4 | 6 | 7 | ♥ | 8 | 9 | 10 |
| 13 | | | 15 | 16 | 17 |
| 11 | 20 | 21 | 22 | 23 | 24 |
| 16 | 27 | | | | |

For every Dick
and Jane and Jerry,
a special day
in February
is a time to win,
a time to woo,
a time for saying,
"I love you,"
with valentines

BEE . . .
mine!

Be my Valentine

both comical and serious
and . . .

*messages mysterious!*

So Brother turned
a little pale
when he saw
in one day's mail,
a piece addressed
to "Brother Bear."
All that he
could do was stare.

Something truly
was amiss.
It said, "S.W.A.K." —
*sealed with a kiss!*

His pale gave way
to a sudden rush
of blood that caused
a mighty blush!

And what it said
inside was worse.
It had this
lovey-dovey verse:

"Oh, Brother Bear,
will you be mine?
From Honey Bear,
your super-secret
valentine!"

OH,
BROTHER
BEAR
WILL YOU BE MINE?
FROM HONEY BEAR
YOUR
SUPER-SECRET
VALENTINE

"Honey Bear?" he wondered.
"Who can that be?
Who could have sent
this **object** to me?"

"A secret admirer,"
Brother Bear said,
"is something I need
like a hole in the head!"

Then he looked at the thing, with its picture of cupid shooting love's dart,

saw that no one was looking and placed the object next to his heart!

"How's the ice?" asked Papa
when Brother came in.
"Is it okay,
or is it too thin?"

"The ice?" said Brother.
"The *hockey* ice!" said Papa.
"The season's about to begin!"

"Oh, *that* ice," said Brother,
distracted by the valentine.
"Conditions for hockey
are perfectly fine."

BEAR COUNTRY
COUSINS PLAY
TODAY

Now it just so happened
that later that day,
Brother Bear's team
was scheduled to play.

Brother dressed for the game
with something like dread,
as he thought of the schedule
that lay ahead.

For as he pulled his jersey
over his woollies,
he knew today's winning team
would eventually meet . . .

THE BEARTOWN BULLIES!

"Just look at him," said Pa,
"takes after his dad.
Reminds me of me
when I was a lad.
You should have seen
me in my prime.

I could skate like lightning

and turn on a dime.

"My slapshot was famous.

When it whizzed through the air,
it was, 'Hold on to your helmet!'
and 'Goalie beware!'"

Brother was impressed
by Papa Bear's shot.
Small Sister Bear,
however, was not.

Enough of hockey!

"I've got slapshots
and pucks
coming out of my ears!
It's all right for them.
But it bores me to tears.

Now I don't object
to hockey as such
but day after day,
it does get to be
a little bit much.

A few hours later
on that day,
star forward Brother
had a game to play.
Sportscaster Joe,
take it away!

Sportscaster Joe, here.
As expected, star forward
Brother Bear has dominated
today's game.

He drives down
the ice. Is checked.
He passes off.

Takes a return pass . . .

Shoots . . .
AND SCORES!

COUSINS 5
VISITORS 0

The final score
was five to zero,
with high-scoring Brother,
the hockey hero!

The cheers for the Cousins
were long and loud.
They left the ice
to the roar of the crowd.

So there you have it.
A stellar performance
by Brother Bear and
another victory for
the Bear Country
Cousins. This puts the
Cousins in the big
Valentine's game
against . . .
the Beartown Bullies—

*a dubious privilege at best.*

TWO-FOUR SIX-EIGHT!

There was a special cheer for Brother as well. The cheerleaders gave him a well-deserved yell.

WHO DO WE APPRECIATE?

BROTHER! BROTHER! NO OTHER!

BROTHER! BROTHER! NO OTHER!

YAAAAY!

They then addressed Brother
in more *personal* terms.

OH-H-H!
SIGH-H-H!
OH MY-Y-Y!

Yuck, when it
comes to mush,
I'd rather eat worms.

And after the game,
making the scene,
was that gorgeous creature,
the lovely Charlene.

Charlene

When, "Very good game,"
she sweetly said,
Brother turned color
from his toes to his head.

"Say! Could she be Honey Bear?
Could it possibly be?
Could she be the one
with a crush on me?"

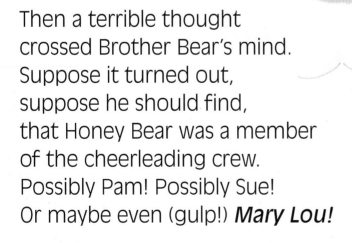

Then a terrible thought
crossed Brother Bear's mind.
Suppose it turned out,
suppose he should find,
that Honey Bear was a member
of the cheerleading crew.
Possibly Pam! Possibly Sue!
Or maybe even (gulp!) *Mary Lou!*

Meanwhile back at the mailbox,
the plot was thickening.
The valentine pace
was rapidly quickening.
Still another valentine
awaited Brother there.
It first caught the eye
of small Sister Bear.

It was flowery and pink
and smelled of perfume.
It increased Brother's feeling
of Valentine's doom.
It was even mushier
than the one before.
As far as he was concerned,
this thing called "love"
was a terrible, awful,
sickening bore.

"And as I said before
in no uncertain terms,
when it comes to mush,
I would rather eat worms.

"Down with mush!
Kissin' and huggin'
and all that slush!
Snuggle buggin'!
And I've no crush
on any member
of the opposite sex
(whatever that is).

I say a hex
on rubbin' noses
or holdin' hands,
or any sort
of long-range plans.

Down with mush!
Whisp'rin' and gigglin'
and all that gush.
Wigglin' and jigglin'.
And I say hush
to any and every mention of
that embarrassing, harassing
thing called . . .
LOVE!"

A little bit later,
when push came to shove,
Brother was on a mission
that was not about love.

He was scouting the Bullies
of Beartown fame,
that his team would play
in the championship game.

He knew just where to find them:
in the fog of Bullies' Creek,
and hidden by the fog,
he took a cautious peek.

"Hmm," said Brother Bear.
"This has to be the place."
But there was no sign
of Bullies,
not a single trace.

And then they came,
out of the mist,
bunched together
like a giant fist.

There were slashing sticks!
A flashing puck!
There was no place to hide!
No way to duck!
Then with Brother looking
for a tree to climb,
the Bullies pulled up.
They scratch-stopped
on a dime.

Their goalie decided
to let Brother live.
Why? Because they had
a demonstration to give.

There was no question,
the Bullies were
powerful opposition.
They were especially strong
at the goalie position.

It was quite a demonstration.
Not a single shot got through.
Brother slunk away.
What to do? What to do?

But as Brother
weighed their chances
in the upcoming game
against the mighty Bullies
of Beartown fame,

he forgot about the other
Valentine's game.
The one in which "LOVE"
is the name of the game.

The *third* Valentine
was a big red heart,
covered all over
with kisses and art.

And at that very moment
with the Honey Bear mystery
getting deeper and deeper,
and the valentine suspense
getting steeper and steeper,
who should ride by,
right there and then,
but the lovely Charlene,
that Bear Country "10."

Then, with a friendly wave
and a whispery "Hi,"
the lovely Charlene
just biked on by.

"Could Charlene be the one?
Could it really be?
Could the lovely Charlene
have a crush on me?"

Valentine's Day—
the day of the match
for the championship.
Bears had come from miles around!
Why, even Bigpaw made the trip.

Brother was suiting up
with the other lads,
putting on
his skates and pads,
when that *other* game
asserted itself
in another envelope
on his locker shelf.

*You shall know me
very soon!
I reveal myself
this afternoon.
signed Honey Bear*

Brother tried being angry,
frustrated, furious.
But he just couldn't manage it.
He was much too curious.

He scanned the stands,
surveyed the scene,
and got a smile
for his trouble
from, yes, you guessed it,
the lovely Charlene.

Then came the cheers
of the cheerleading crew.
We musn't forget
the cheerleading crew—
consisting of Pam and Sue
and (gulp!) *Mary Lou*.

He is checked hard!
Oh, these Bullies are tough.

Brother recovers, takes a return pass, and shoots!

An easy save for the Bullies' super goalie.

BROTHER! BROTHER! NO-OTHER!

KNIT ONE! PURL TWO! COUNTRY COUSINS WOO! WOO!

Yes, folks, this match is everything we hoped it would be: Bullies' power against the Cousins' speed. Star forward Brother Bear against the Bullies' super goalie with the Bullies leading one to zero and just minutes to play. It begins to look like another Bullies' year. And Brother looks a little discouraged and who can blame him. But wait!

There was no doubt.
Brother was tired.
So, in an effort to get
his engine refired,
he looked in the stands
for the lovely Charlene.
But when he found her,
his disappointment was keen.

Because the Cousins were losing,
Charlene had switched sides.
Charlene was lovely.
But she was as changeable
as the tides.

Brother saw red.
He reached for the puck.
And whether by skill
or pure dumb luck,
he shot . . .
AND SCORED!

The crowd went wild.
The score was now tied.
The Bullies were tough.
But the Cousins were working
on anger and pride.

BULLIES 1
COUSINS 1

A final face-off.
A fight for the puck.

Brother checked by a Bully
as big as a truck.

A desperate shot.
But it went wide.

A slip to the ice.
A pinwheeling slide.

A reach for the puck.
A terrific get—

And somehow that puck slipped into the net.

THE COUSINS WIN!
THE COUSINS WIN!
THE COUSINS WIN!

The cheers for the Cousins were long and loud. But Brother continued to search the crowd, for some signal, some sign, of Honey Bear, his super-secret valentine.

Then as Brother reached
for the last handshake,
something happened
to boggle the mind.
The Bullies' great goalie,
who had been sort of
lingering behind,
began to take off her mask and pads.
That's right—HER mask and pads!

Brother was shocked—
utterly stunned.
The goalie who'd stopped
all those shots he had gunned
**was a she!**
It said so right there,
on the extra-large T-shirt
of Miss Honey Bear.

Then the Bullies' super goalie
said to star forward Brother,
"Maybe we could practice
with each other.
I can practice my save
and you could practice your shot."
Brother grinned from ear to ear,
reached out his hand and said,
"WHY . . . NOT?"

They became fast friends,
right then and there,
star forward Brother
and Miss Honey Bear.

# •ABOUT THE AUTHORS•

Stan and Jan Berenstain have been writing and illustrating books about bears for more than thirty years. In 1962, their self-proclaimed "mom and pop operation" began producing one of the most popular children's book series of all time — *The Berenstain Bears*. Since then, children the world over have followed Mama Bear, Papa Bear, Sister Bear, and Brother Bear on over 100 adventures through books, cassettes, and animated television specials.

Stan and Jan Berenstain live in Bucks County, Pennsylvania. They have two sons, Michael and Leo, and four grandchildren.

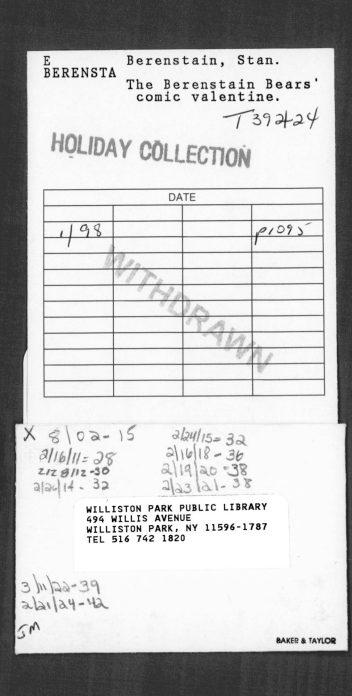